I0788096

Sam and the Cave of Fear

WRITTEN AND ILLUSTRATED BY MR. JOE LUCIANO

This is Sam, he is your average boy. One night, Sam had an unusual nightmare that would cause him to wake up screaming and crying for his parents. This did not just happen once, but many nights, between midnight and two am.

Hi

His parents became very concerned. They tried different things to help Sam sleep through the night. They tried playing soft music, reading happy stories, and even took Sam to the doctor, but nothing was helping. The nightmare continued.

The Great
green
green ham

One Sunday after church, Sam asked his parents about Jesus. He asked, "Did the winds and the waves really obey him?" His parents smiled and said, "Yes, but not just the winds and the waves, also fig trees and demons would obey him." Then Sam asked, "Do you think nightmares will obey him too?" They said, "Yes!"

Then Sam's Dad said, "We will pray to-night before bed to ask Jesus to help you to overcome this nightmare." That night Sam's Dad prayed with him. As his Dad tucked him into bed, he told Sam, "When you are in the nightmare, if you call on the name of Jesus, he will help you."

That night Sam had the nightmare, and it went like this ... He appeared in a dark creepy cave, so dark, he could barely see in front of him. The fear gripped him like a tight bear-hug. Despite the fear, Sam started to walk deeper into the cave.

From the walls, a scary ugly creature jumped out, and growled at him. Sam remembered what his Dad told him to do. With his eyes closed, he shouted out the name of, "JESUS!" As he did, the scary, ugly creature vanished, and a torch appeared on the floor of the cave. Sam picked it up.

Jesus

As he held the torch up to see where to go, he noticed it was pointing in a specific direction. Sam followed the way the torch was pointing.

As he did, another creepy, scary creature jumped out growling at him. Sam called out the name of Jesus, and a gust of wind blew the scary creature away. Sam continued on the pathway the torch was pointing out.

Growl
Jesus

Before Sam knew it, he saw light shining in the distance. He knew it was the exit of the cave. The closer he got to the exit, the flame of the torch started to get smaller. Then he noticed a figure of a man standing outside the cave. The torch went out, waking him up, with the sun shining on his bed.

Sam rolled over to the edge of the bed, and grabbed his bible off the floor. He opened it up to Luke 8:22-25 and read...

Sam
Bible
Bible

One day Jesus and his disciples got into a boat to go across to the other side of the lake. As they were sailing along Jesus fell asleep.

As he slept, the wind rose becoming a fierce, violent storm upon the lake. The storm caused the lake to throw the boat around, and waves to crash upon it, threatening to capsize it. The disciples be-came fearful, and woke up Jesus saying, "Master, Master, we're sinking! Don't you care that we are going to drown?"

Z Z Z
Master!

With great authority Jesus rebuked the howling wind and surging waves, and instantly they stopped and the lake became as smooth as glass. Then Jesus said to his disciples, "Why are you fearful? Have you lost your faith in me?" Shocked and shaken they said with amazement to one another, "Who is this man who has authority over the winds and the waves that they obey him?"

Who is this that the winds and the waves obey Him!

Then Sam closed his bible and smiled. Now he knows who the figure was at the end of the cave.

The End

THREE YEARS LATER...

To be Continued